THE
FARAWAY
WOODS

THE
BEYOND

For NOAH, MASON, BRODY & ETHAN

About This Book: The illustrations for this book were done in pencil, scanned textures, and digital paint. This book was edited by Deirdre Jones and designed by Véronique Lefèvre Sweet. The production was supervised by Erika Schwartz, and the production editor was Jen Graham. The text was set in Billy, and the display type is Nanami HM Book.

Copyright © 2020 by Chad Otis • Cover illustration copyright © 2020 by Chad Otis • Cover design by Véronique Lefèvre Sweet • Cover copyright © 2020 by Hachette Book Group, Inc. • Hachette Book Group supports the right to free expression and the value of copyright. The purpose of copyright is to encourage writers and artists to produce the creative works that enrich our culture. • The scanning, uploading, and distribution of this book without permission is a theft of the author's intellectual property. If you would like permission to use material from the book (other than for review purposes), please contact permissions@hbgusa.com. Thank you for your support of the author's rights. • Little, Brown and Company • Hachette Book Group • 1290 Avenue of the Americas, New York, NY 10104 • Visit us at LBYR.com • First Edition: August 2020 • Little, Brown and Company is a division of Hachette Book Group, Inc. The Little, Brown name and logo are trademarks of Hachette Book Group, Inc. • The publisher is not responsible for websites (or their content) that are not owned by the publisher. • Library of Congress Cataloging-in-Publication Data • Names: Otis, Chad, author, illustrator. • Title: Oliver the curious owl / Chad Otis. • Description: First edition. | New York : Little, Brown and Company, 2020. | Summary: A curious owl and a friendly bug ask questions that lead them on a grand adventure away from—and back to—their home tree. • Identifiers: LCCN 2018060494| ISBN 9780316529877 (hardcover) | ISBN 9780316529860 (ebook) | ISBN 9780316529853 (library edition ebook) • Subjects: | CYAC: Curiosity—Fiction. | Questions and answers—Fiction. | Friendship—Fiction. | Owls—Fiction. | Insects—Fiction. • Classification: LCC PZ7.1.O77 Ol 2020 | DDC [E]—dc23 • LC record available at https://lccn.loc.gov/2018060494 • ISBNs: 978-0-316-52987-7 (hardcover), 978-0-316-52986-0 (ebook), 978-0-316-52988-4 (ebook), 978-0-316-52983-9 (ebook) • PRINTED IN CHINA • APS • 10 9 8 7 6 5 4 3 2 1

Oliver
the Curious Owl

Chad Otis

LB

Little, Brown and Company

New York Boston

The owl family had everything they needed in their big tree.

It was very quiet and very safe, so they never ventured far.

The only question they ever asked was "Who?"

But Oliver was new to the family,
and he asked lots of other questions.

Soon Oliver knew the answer to every question he had about being an owl. Now he wanted to learn about life *outside* the big tree.

Then one day he met someone else who asked lots of questions.

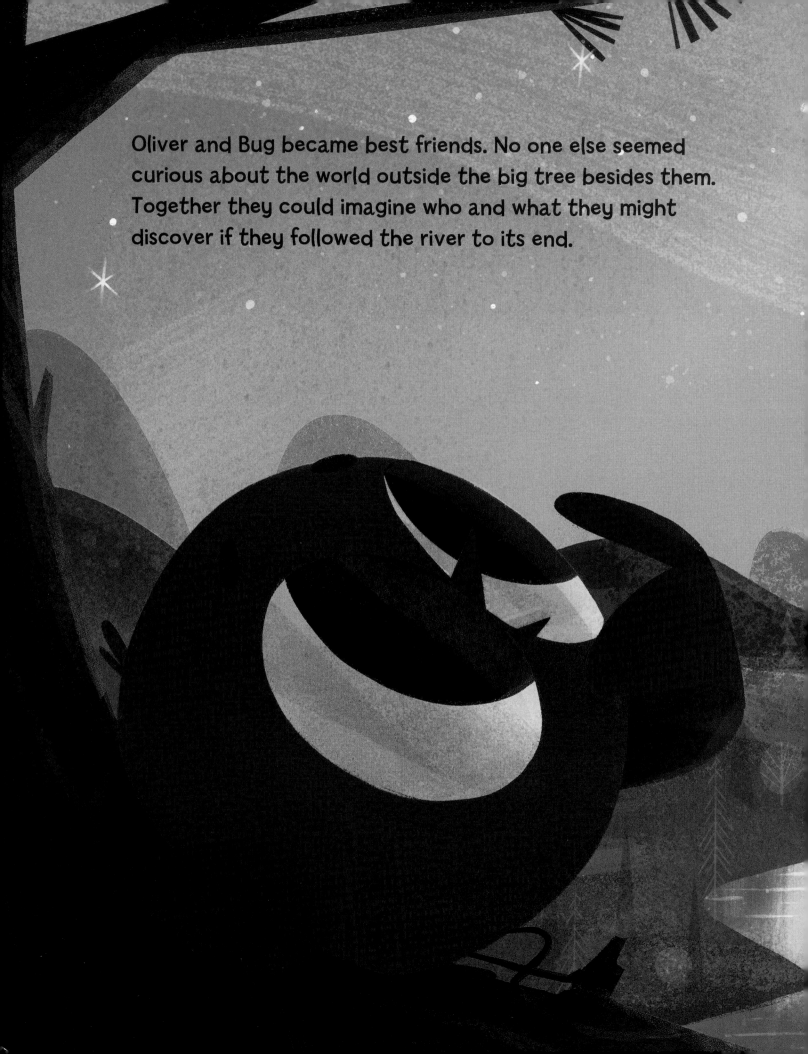

Oliver and Bug became best friends. No one else seemed curious about the world outside the big tree besides them. Together they could imagine who and what they might discover if they followed the river to its end.

But every time Bug suggested they go exploring,
Oliver decided it was safer to stay home. He was
afraid they might get lost.

Then one night...

SNAP!

Bug

fell

into

the river

and was quickly swept far from the big tree.

Oliver didn't know what to do! He paced, he hopped, he chirp-chirp-chirped.

And then...

...he leaped from the big tree

and chased after his friend.

When Oliver reached the faraway woods, he was surrounded by strange new things.

Oliver raced toward his friend as fast as he could!

He swooped down and scooped Bug up just in time.

They burst from the cool darkness of the woods—it was the end of the river! And it was more incredible than they had imagined.

Oliver and Bug were very far from home, but they couldn't stop now!

They made new friends,

tried new things,

explored new places,

even ate new foods!

Now they were very *very* far from home.

And they'd never had so much fun in their lives.

Suddenly the sky turned dark.

Lightning flashed and thunder rumbled.

The wind twisted and the rain fell harder.

Everything looked strange and different.

They were lost!

Oliver began to think maybe they shouldn't have explored all day—or gone so far from home. Maybe they should have stayed in their safe big tree.

But then Bug had an idea!

Eep!

If they followed all the

whos...

whats...

whens...

wheres...

and whys

they had asked that day, it might lead them back to...

...the big tree!

It was strange—the big tree
didn't seem quite so big now.

Oliver's family had been very worried. They hugged him tight and told him never to leave home again.

But that night, Oliver and Bug told their family all about the amazing world they had discovered beyond the big tree.

And they said they would be very sad if they never got to see it again.

So the next day...

...everyone followed Oliver and Bug.

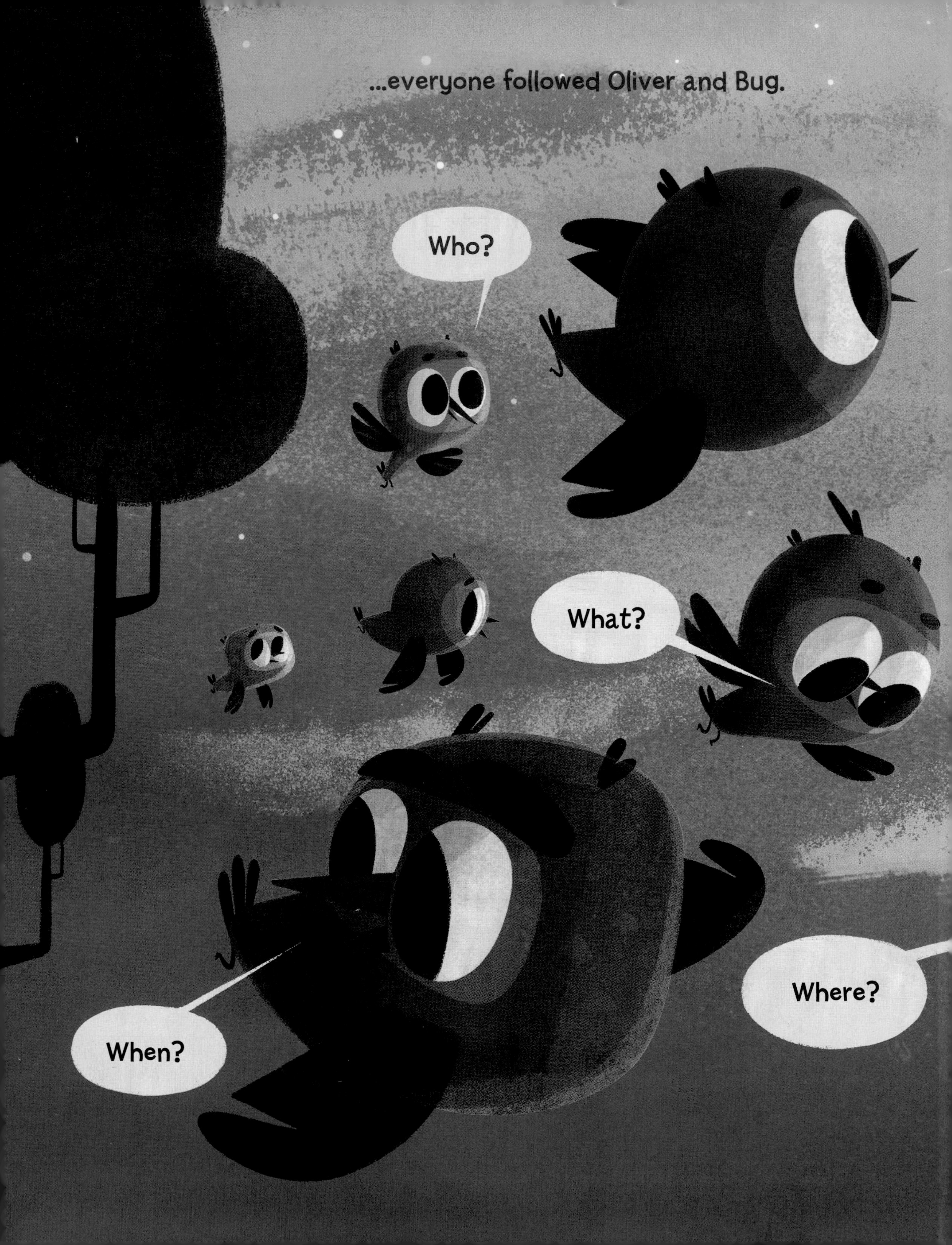

They had *lots* of questions.

THE
BIG TREE

Are you curious about the animals in this book?

 BATS HANG UPSIDE DOWN because it's easier for them to start flying from this position. Bats do most of their hunting at night, when it's hard to see, so they make high-pitched squeaking noises and wait for the echoes to come back to their big ears, telling them where to find food.

BEAVERS REALLY DO EAT WOOD, but only small branches, bark, and twigs. Their teeth never stop growing, and chewing wood prevents their teeth from getting too large. It also keeps their teeth sharp, which helps beavers cut down trees to build dams and lodges.

 ALLIGATORS DON'T CHEW THEIR FOOD. Even though they have lots of teeth, alligators use them to grab prey—then swallow it whole! Alligators hunt mostly at night, and they have special eyes that reflect light to help them see in the dark. It sometimes looks like their eyes are glowing!